Spooksville

THE DARK CORNER

Christopher Pike

a division of Hodder Headline plc

First published in the USA in 1995
as an Archway Paperback by Pocket Books,
a division of Simon & Schuster Inc.

First published in Great Britain in 1996
by Hodder Children's Books

10 9 8 7 6 5 4 3 2

A Catalogue record for this book is available from the British Library

ISBN 0 340 66119 4

Typeset by Avon Dataset Ltd, Bidford-on-Avon, Warks.

Printed and bound in Great Britain by
Cox & Wyman Ltd, Reading, Berks.

Hodder Children's Books
a division of Hodder Headline plc
338 Euston Road
London NW1 3BH

One

It was Sally Wilcox who brought up how cool Bryce Poole was, and started the argument that led to another trip through the Secret Path. Of course later she swore she had nothing to do with what happened. It was a typical situation in Spooksville. No one ever wanted to be blamed for starting another adventure, at least not in the middle of the adventure – when it looked like they would all die.

The day started as so many did that summer. Adam Freeman, Cindy Makey, Sally Wilcox and Watch got together for a breakfast of milk and doughnuts. While stuffing their faces at the local coffee shop, they tried to figure out what to do with the day.

'Only a few weeks and we'll be back in school,' Sally said. 'We have to make the most of every day.'

'I'm kind of looking forward to going back to

school,' Cindy said. 'I like learning new things.'

'Summer vacation in Spooksville is more of a learning experience than any schooling,' Sally muttered.

'What is school like here?' Adam asked. 'Is it as weird as the rest of the town?'

'It's pretty normal,' Watch said.

'Except for a few of the teachers,' Sally added. 'Not all of them are human.'

'How did I know you were going to say that?' Cindy asked.

'We do have a couple of unusual teachers,' Watch admitted.

Sally nodded. 'There's Mr Castro. He teaches history, basically. But sometimes he talks about the future.'

'Don't say it,' Cindy interrupted. 'Mr Castro's really from the future.'

'Well, he's not from around here,' Watch said.

'I think he was built at the North Pole,' Sally said. 'If my sources are accurate.'

'I heard it was the South Pole,' Watch said.

Adam and Cindy exchanged looks. 'So he's a robot?' Adam asked.

'He's not a desktop computer,' Sally said.

Watch spoke reluctantly. 'He does seem to have several mechanical qualities. For example, he never eats lunch. He never drinks water. When he's tired, he lies out on the football field and soaks up the sun's rays. That's how he supposedly recharges his batteries.'

'He also has a hearing aid that looks more like a cosmic receiver,' Sally said. 'He never takes it off. I hear it's wired directly into his positronic brain.' She added, 'He sure doesn't have trouble hearing.'

Cindy shook her head. 'I don't believe any of this.'

'Wait till you get him for history,' Sally said. 'And he pops his eyes out in the middle of a lecture just to clean his contact lenses.'

'You said a couple of teachers were weird,' Adam said. 'Who's the other one?'

'Mrs Fry,' Sally said. 'She teaches biology. She's a snake.'

'She has scaly skin?' Cindy asked.

'Yes,' Sally said impatiently. 'I told you, she's a snake. When have you ever seen a snake that didn't have scaly skin?'

'What Sally means is Mrs Fry seems to be part snake,' Watch said. 'She slides around the room and hisses all the time. Some people think she's a descendant of a reptilian race that lived in this area millions of years ago.'

'You dissect frogs all the time in her class,' Sally said. 'But never snakes or lizards. And all the frog parts disappear between classes. She eats them all.'

Cindy made a face. 'That's gross.'

'You haven't seen gross until you've seen Mrs Fry shed her skin,' Sally said.

Adam didn't know what to make of any of this. 'It sounds like it's going to be an interesting school year.'

Sally brightened. 'There are some cute guys at school.'

Cindy was cautious. 'Are they all human?'

Sally waved her hand. 'There's this one guy, his name's Bryce Poole, and he's so cool. He's like a young James Bond. Nothing disturbs him. You'll adore him, Cindy. He's got real dark hair, and super warm brown eyes. He's only twelve but he doesn't act like a kid. He talks like a well-read sophisticated adult – like me.'

Cindy was interested. 'How come we haven't seen him this summer?'

'He's a loner,' Sally said in a confidential tone. 'He takes his own risks and he doesn't go whining to anyone about the consequences.'

'It's hard to imagine someone who's taken more

risks than us this summer,' Adam muttered.

'And I can't remember that we ever whined to anyone,' Watch added.

Sally stopped and laughed. 'Are you guys jealous of Bryce?'

Adam shrugged. 'How can I be jealous of someone I've never met?'

'I've met him and he's no big deal,' Watch said.

'What bothers you guys more?' Sally persisted. 'Is it his obvious intelligence? His smouldering looks? Or is it his dynamic attitude?'

'I told you,' Adam said. 'I've never met the guy. I know nothing about him.'

'I'm trying to tell you about him,' Sally said. 'And you're getting all upset.' She paused. 'I think you're jealous, but you don't have to be. I like him as a friend. There's nothing between us.'

'I bet he's wonderful,' Cindy gushed.

'How can you say that?' Adam demanded. 'You haven't met him either.'

'But if Cindy does fall in love with him when she meets him,' Sally said, 'you mustn't stand in her way, Adam. You have to be mature about it. So Bryce is better looking and smarter than you or Watch. It doesn't mean you're not both worthy human beings.'

'Oh boy,' Adam muttered.

'Where's a good place to meet him?' Cindy asked.

Sally spoke seriously. 'You have to catch him coming and going. He never stays in one place long. He's always taking some super risk to protect this town from danger.'

'Hold on a second,' Adam said. 'Since I've been here, what has he done to protect this town? I mean, we've had to deal with aliens, the Haunted Cave, the Cold People, not to mention the Witch. Where was he all this time?'

'Yeah,' Watch agreed. 'Bryce didn't even bother to help us out with the Howling Ghost.'

Sally smiled condescendingly. 'Bryce doesn't deal with small crises. He only handles the major ones.'

'How can you call the Cold People a small crisis?' Adam demanded. 'If we hadn't stopped them, they would have taken over the whole planet.'

'Yes, but this isn't that big a planet,' Sally said. 'Not compared to the rest of the galaxy. Bryce deals more with cosmic emergencies.'

Adam and Watch looked at each other and rolled their eyes. 'Like what?' Adam asked. 'What is this big shot Bryce doing right now to protect us?'

Sally glanced around the coffee shop to make sure

no one was listening. She spoke in a hushed tone. 'Bryce is working with the Secret Path. He's trying to halt the interdimensional flow of negativity so that it doesn't seep into our reality.'

Adam frowned. 'How do you know this?'

Sally sat back and nodded gravely. 'I have my sources.'

'I don't believe it,' Watch said. 'Bryce Poole doesn't even know what the Secret Path is. I asked him about it before talking to Bum and he didn't even know where it began.'

'He was just acting like he didn't know,' Sally said. 'He told me later after I told him about our adventures on the other side. He didn't think you were equipped enough to survive the dangers of the interdimensional portal.'

It was Watch's turn to frown. 'Equipped with what?'

'I don't want to get personal here,' Sally said.

'You are always personal,' Adam said drily.

Sally was offended. 'Don't take it out on me that Cindy is suddenly interested in another guy.'

'I didn't say that exactly,' Cindy said.

'Your voice said it all,' Sally said. 'And I understand what Adam's going through. I'm sympathetic. To experience raging jealousy and bitter rejection for the first time is not easy.'

Adam sighed. 'I am so grateful for your sympathy.'

'We're arguing about nothing,' Watch said. 'Bryce isn't a super-hero. He's probably not even using the Secret Path.'

'How do you know?' Sally shot back. 'You've been afraid to use it since that first time.'

'I haven't been afraid,' Watch said. 'I have just been busy with other things.'

'Yeah, like saving the planet with his best friend,' Adam added.

'I saved the planet too,' Sally said.

'Then you and Bryce should be perfect together,' Adam said.

Sally laughed. 'You are so jealous!'

Adam got angry. 'Why should I be jealous of a guy who thinks he's James Bond? I agree with Watch. This guy is not using the Secret Path. He doesn't have the guts.'

Sally stood. 'Why don't we go and see?'

'Go where?' Cindy asked. 'See what?'

'The Secret Path starts or ends in the cemetery,' Sally said, 'depending on how you look at it. Why don't we go there now and look for signs of Bryce? Then we can see who the real hero in this town is.'

'Why would Bryce leave signs that he's using the Secret Path?' Watch asked.

'Yeah,' Adam said. 'Who is he trying to impress?'

'You guys have an answer for everything.' Sally sniggered and turned for the door. 'Are you chickens coming or not?'

The way she worded the question, it was really impossible to say no.

Two

At the cemetery they had no trouble finding Madeline Templeton's tombstone. It was larger than all the other stones, and it had a large black raven carved on the top. The bird glared down at them and Adam was reminded of the last time they had taken the path, and the horror they had experienced on the other side. He shuddered as he glanced round the cemetery. The place was dismal. The few naked trees stood like angry skeletons. A shadow seemed to hang across the dry grounds, although there wasn't a cloud in the sky.

'Did you put this here?' Watch asked Sally as he knelt by Madeline Templeton's tombstone. He held up a green knapsack. Sally took a step forward and shook her head.

'No,' she said. 'Why would I put anything here? It probably belongs to Bryce.'

'How convenient,' Adam said.

Sally ignored him. 'What does it have inside it?' she asked.

Watch opened the sack. 'Binoculars. A thermos of water. A compass. A few flares.' He held up a hunting knife. 'It looks as if Bryce was anticipating trouble.'

'But why would he leave his equipment here?' Cindy asked.

'I don't know,' Watch said.

'I don't understand something,' Cindy said. 'How do you get through this Secret Path? You guys said something about walking backwards into the tombstone?'

'It's not that easy,' Adam explained. 'First you have to trace a route all over Spooksville. Then you have to walk from the front gate of the cemetery backwards into the tombstone.'

'Can't you just walk backwards into the tombstone,' Cindy asked, 'and forget the other stuff?'

'No,' Watch said. 'I tried it once not long ago and it didn't work. First you have to visit the location of each of the significant events in Madeline Templeton's life. You have to go to each place in order. Somehow that opens the portal to other dimensions.'

'Then Bryce must have done that?' Cindy asked.

'I'm not convinced this stuff belongs to Bryce,' Adam interrupted. 'It doesn't have his name on it.'

'You simply refuse to accept the fact that he is using the Secret Path,' Sally said.

'What are we arguing about here?' Watch said, before another argument could break out. 'It's possible Bryce is using the Secret Path. I admit that much now. But so what? What does it have to do with us?'

'Nothing,' Sally said simply. 'I was merely trying to make the point that Bryce is braver than you guys.'

'Oh boy,' Adam muttered.

'Well you haven't gone back through the path,' Sally said. 'But he has, many times.'

'The Secret Path is dangerous,' Adam said. 'If he's dumb enough to keep using it, then that's his problem.'

'It is only dangerous if you're not strong enough to handle it,' Sally said.

'I can't believe you just said that,' Adam said. 'You were the one who was against us using it in the first place.'

'Wait a second,' Watch said. 'Sally does have a point. Remember what Bum told us when he spoke about the path. He said, "The Secret Path doesn't always lead to the same place. It all depends on you. If you're a little scared, you end up in a place that's a little scary. If you're terrified, the path is like a road to terror." '

'I'm sure Bryce is able to control his fear,' Sally said. 'And go where he wishes.'

'Good for him,' Adam said sarcastically.

'I'm not saying you should follow him,' Sally said.

'We don't have to do that,' Watch agreed.

'I mean, you don't have to try to impress me,' Sally said. 'I like you guys the way you are. I don't care how brave you are. Do you care, Cindy?'

'No,' Cindy replied. But then she considered. 'But I would like to meet this guy.'

'He's a real hero,' Sally said.

Adam and Watch looked at each other and it would be safe to say they each looked pretty disgusted.

'Do you feel like she's trying to push us on to the path again?' Adam asked.

'It feels like it,' Watch said.

'Why do you think?' Adam asked, ignoring the girls for a moment.

'I think, personally, that she's worried Bryce is trapped on the other side of the Secret Path,' Watch said. 'I think she wants us to go and rescue him, but she's too proud to say it outright.'

'My thoughts exactly,' Adam said.

Sally didn't protest. They had hit a nerve with her. For a moment she stared at the wicked tombstone, then she lowered her head.

'He's been gone a while,' she said finally.

'How do you know?' Cindy asked.

'He told me he was going,' Sally said quietly. 'That was a week ago. I haven't seen him since.'

'Is this his knapsack?' Watch asked. 'Why did he leave it on this side?'

Sally shrugged. 'I think it's his. I don't know why he didn't take it with him.'

'Why was he using the path?' Adam asked.

'I told you the truth on that point,' Sally said. 'He said he had to stop the overflow of evil into our dimension.'

'At least he sets his sights high,' Adam remarked.

'If we're going to use the Secret Path, we have to start now,' Watch said, checking one of his four watches, which he always wore. 'It takes half the day to visit all the important places in Madeline Templeton's life.'

'Wait a second,' Adam said. 'Before we go to all that trouble we have to decide if we even *can* help Bryce. There's no reason to think if we step through the path we'll end up in the same dimension as him. We might end up back where we were last time, and that's one place I don't want to see again.'

'But if he is trapped,' Sally said, 'how can you just leave him to an eternity of torment and agony?'

'Better him than us,' Watch said wisely.

Adam put his hand on Sally's shoulder. 'You're really worried about him, aren't you? That was just a show at the coffee shop, wasn't it? You've been trying to bully us into taking the path.'

Sally nodded. 'He's never been gone this long before. I'll go with you guys if you go.' She paused. 'I'm not afraid.'

'Yeah, you are,' Watch said. 'We're all afraid to try the path again, and we can't just talk ourselves out of our fear. And that means if we do take it, we'll probably end up in a scary place.'

Sally nodded as she stared up at the tombstone. 'In an evil place, where Bryce went.'

Three

The sequence they had taken before to get on to the Secret Path had been:

1. The beach (where Madeline was supposedly born).
2. Derby Tree (where Madeline cursed the tree and turned its leaves red).
3. A cave (where Madeline killed a lion with her bare hands).
4. The chapel (where Madeline got married).
5. The reservoir (where Madeline drowned her husband).
6. The beach (where Madeline was almost burned to death).
7. The cemetery (where Madeline was buried).

Obviously going to the beach twice seemed stupid, but the sequence, they knew, was the key. Going to the cave and then to the chapel and then back to the reservoir was also inconvenient, since the caves were not far from the reservoir. But they stuck to what they had done before because it had worked.

It was close to four o'clock by the time they got back to the cemetery. Starting at the front gate, they began to walk backwards towards the tombstone, holding hands.

'Why do we have to do this?' Cindy asked, sounding nervous.

'Because Madeline Templeton was carried here upside down,' Adam said. 'This is our symbolic way of re-enacting that event.' He paused. 'You sound scared.'

'I am scared,' Cindy said quickly. 'I've never gone through an interdimensional portal before.'

'We're really going to end up in a horrible place,' Sally muttered.

'Maybe you shouldn't go with us,' Adam said to Cindy. 'You could stand guard on this side.'

'What am I guarding?' Cindy asked, sounding interested.

'You never know what might come back through the portal,' Sally said.

'It might be a good idea if one of us does stay on this

side,' Watch said. 'If we don't return, that person could go for help.' He added, 'I don't mind standing guard.'

Sally glanced over her shoulder at the approaching tombstone. 'I bet none of us would mind staying at this point.' But then she suddenly let go of Cindy's hand. 'But it should be Cindy. The rest of us are experienced with this portal.'

'Are you guys sure?' Cindy asked, also letting go of Adam's hand, watching them as they continued to trudge backwards towards the grave. 'I don't mind staying behind.'

'You're the logical choice to stay,' Adam said, trying to reassure her. 'There's no use going through the portal if you don't want to do it.'

'Like we're all having a barrel of fun here,' Sally remarked.

Cindy walked beside them as they stumbled backwards. 'I feel like a coward.'

'You should,' Sally said. 'But I'll try not to bother you about it.' She paused. 'If Bryce should reappear before we do, send him looking for us.'

'Have him bring his knife,' Watch said.

'No,' Adam said. 'Cindy, grab the knapsack. I want to bring his stuff with us.'

Cindy hurried to the tombstone and grabbed the

bag. She handed it to Adam as the gang neared the wall of stone.

'How long should I wait here before I go for help?' she asked.

'If we're not back by dark,' Watch said, 'find Bum, tell him what's happened. He might be able to help.'

'If he can be bothered,' Sally added.

'We're just about there,' Adam said anxiously. 'Let's hold on to each other tightly. Goodbye, Cindy. Wish us luck.'

'Good luck!' Cindy called.

'I feel a whole lot better now that she's blessed us,' Sally said.

They stumbled as they stepped on to the grave site. For a moment Adam thought they would fall on to the Secret Path. Suddenly everything went black and he felt as if he was sinking fast. His friends seemed many miles away. He couldn't see them. He was in the eye of a hurricane, where everything was perfectly calm, for the moment, although he knew madness raged all around him.

Four

When everything returned to normal Adam realised they were in a place that was far from normal. It was Spooksville and it was not. As they looked round in wonder, they realised they were in the heavenly counterpart of home. A sweet scent filled the air. The surrounding trees were a lush green. Everything seemed to be glowing with a faint golden light, radiating love and joy.

'This isn't so bad,' Sally remarked.

'It looks like paradise,' Watch said, removing his glasses to clean them. 'It's amazing we came to such a nice place, what with how scared we all were.'

'I wasn't scared,' Sally said quickly, letting go of their hands. 'I think it was me who lifted our overall vibes.'

'I like how your arms shake so much when you're not scared,' Adam said.

'They only shook because they were holding on to your arms,' Sally said, stepping away from the tombstone. She sucked in a deep breath of the sweet air. 'I love this place! Look at that sky. It looks like one huge rainbow. I don't know if I want to go home.'

Watch was concerned. 'We tried the Secret Path for a purpose, to find Bryce. But if he's off fighting evil, I doubt he's here.'

'That's true,' Adam agreed. Then he stopped and stared down at some initials on the bottom of the tombstone – BP. He pointed them out to the others. 'Bryce Poole. He must have been here.'

Sally bent over the initials. 'It's only a couple of letters, but it looks like his handwriting.' She raised her head and stared out of the cemetery, which actually looked more like a park. 'I wonder where he could have gone?'

'We could walk into town and ask for him,' Watch said, still fiddling with his glasses. 'I think I see people in the distance.'

'Wait a second,' Adam said. 'We should figure out where we are before we talk to anyone.'

'That's easy,' Sally said. 'We're in heaven.'

'You mean we're in *a* heaven,' Adam said. 'This place is beautiful but it's still Spooksville. See, the castle's over there, and the same ocean is down that way.'

'What I mean is we don't have to worry about getting killed here,' Sally said. 'I think if Bryce is around, people will be happy to lead us to him.'

'Then why did he carve his initials on the bottom of the tombstone?' Adam said. 'He could have just set out a sign announcing that he was here.'

'He might have been afraid of something,' Watch agreed.

Sally laughed. 'Nonsense! This is one place I'm not afraid of. Let's go and explore. I think Bryce is here, and that when we find him he'll probably be having the time of his life.'

'I hope you're right,' Adam said.

They got on to the road that wound down towards the sea and the centre of town. Along the way they passed the castle. To their immense surprise they saw Ms Ann Templeton – or at least this dimension's counterpart – supervising a picnic for a bunch of dwarves and elves. She waved as they looked over, and they didn't know what else to do so they waved back. They seemed to be having a barbecue of chicken and fish. Each of the dwarves had a can of Coke in hand, but the elves were all drinking orange soda out of clear glass bottles.

'See,' Sally said. 'Here she doesn't have any of those nasty goblins working for her.'

'I kind of liked Belfart,' Watch mused. 'I hope the Marines accepted him.'

'Maybe we should stop and talk to Ann Templeton,' Adam wondered aloud. 'Get the lowdown on this place.'

'No,' Sally said. 'I want to get into town. Bryce is most likely there.' She added, 'I wouldn't mind going to my house, and seeing what the Sally on this side is like.'

'I don't know if that would be a good idea,' Adam said, although the same thought had occurred to him. 'It might complicate things if we meet ourselves.'

'It might give us a mild case of schizophrenia,' Watch agreed.

'You guys are no fun today,' Sally said. 'I'm dying to meet the heavenly version of myself – no pun intended. I bet I'm simply extraordinary.'

'There is a lot of room for improvement,' Adam muttered.

Sally snorted. 'I heard that. Come on, let's at least get something to eat. I bet the food here is delicious.'

They ended up stopping at a fast food joint on the edge of town. In their normal Spooksville the place was called Fred's Fat Food. But here the place was called Friend's Fantastic Food. Plus the guy at the counter didn't look anything like the original Fred, who had tattoos on his arms and dirty fingernails and an apron stained with human blood. The handsome young man who took their order had long golden locks and eyes as bright blue as the clear sky. In fact, he didn't even want to be paid. He pushed their money back when they set it on the counter. The food was on the house.

'I could get into living here,' Sally said.

'Maybe that's why Bryce didn't return,' Watch said. 'He liked it so much he just decided to stay.'

'Whatever he decided we have to go back,' Adam said. 'Cindy's waiting for us. She'll start to get worried.'

'If she hadn't been such a coward she could be with us here now,' Sally said.

'You thought she should stay,' Adam protested.

'And I'm glad she did,' Sally said. 'She was so scared – we probably all would have ended up in some dark corner of the universe.'

Their food arrived and it was divine. Really, it tasted better than any meal they'd ever had in their lives, and it was just three hot-dogs and chips. Sally was so pleased by the food that she ordered a vanilla milk-shake as well, which she refused to share with Adam.

'You can still get fat in heaven,' she said. 'I wouldn't want that for you if we're going to live forever now.'

When they were about to leave the place, Adam struck up a conversation with the young man who served them. He listened patiently while Adam explained how they were searching for a friend named Bryce Poole. Adam even asked Sally to describe Bryce. When they had finished the man said in a sympathetic tone:

'You three are not from round here, are you?'

'Not exactly,' Adam replied. 'We're sort of from a neighbouring city, if you know what I mean.'

The man nodded. 'I understand. We get people like you now and then.'

'You do?' Sally asked, amazed.

'Yes,' the young man said. 'And the best thing you can do, no matter what the situation, is go find your counterpart in the city. Once you find him or her, everything will be all right.'

'That's exactly what I wanted to do,' Sally said, looking rather pleased with herself.

Watch was confused. 'So you know we're not from this dimension?'

The young man with the golden hair smiled. 'That's obvious to all of us.'

'You mean everyone in the city knows we're strangers here?' Adam asked.

The man ignored the question. 'Find your counterpart and everything will become clear.' He paused and stared off into the distance. As he did so a strange light shone in his eyes. 'I think they're waiting for you at Adam's house.'

'Waiting for us?' Watch asked. 'How do they know we're here?'

The man just smiled again. 'You'd better hurry. You don't want to keep them waiting.'

Feeling confused, Adam left the food place with his friends. Sally was insistent they head straight for Adam's house. But both Watch and Adam were having doubts.

'He didn't really answer our questions,' Watch complained.

'He said our other selves would help us,' Sally replied. 'He was a nice man – we can trust him.'

'He seemed like a nice man,' Adam said. 'But I agree with Watch. He gave vague answers.'

'I don't care what you guys say,' Sally replied. 'I'm going to see my better half. I can hardly wait to have a deep conversation with her.'

'That's one argument she's finally going to lose,' Watch said.

Since they didn't know exactly what was bothering them, Adam and Watch reluctantly agreed to accompany Sally to visit their other halves. Finding Adam's house was not difficult. It was exactly where it was in the other Spooksville.

Their three counterparts were sitting outside Adam's house.

They smiled when they saw them.

All six of them smiled.

Then the counterparts stood and walked towards them.

As they did so, their faces began to change.

They began to melt. Into hideous demon forms.

Five

It was too late. The three demons – they even had horns now – were on them in an instant. Adam was struck across the face with a scaly hand. His arms were yanked behind his back. He felt a sharp pain in his spine and dropped Bryce Poole's knapsack. For a moment everything went black and he thought he would pass out. Then he realised he was being dragged towards a steel pole, which he had not noticed a second ago. It stood in the centre of his garden, spiked chains hanging from its side.

The garden was no longer the same. All round them the scenery was changing, becoming darker and dirtier, lit with a chilling red glow. It was as if the heavenly version of Spooksville was turning into a hellish realm. The demon that had hold of Adam leered in his face. The creature's teeth were sharp, his eyes like those of a wicked cat, green and splintered with thick red veins. The nails on his claws were like razors. He hissed at Adam.

'We have you now, fool!' the demon said as he snapped Adam's wrists into cuffs attached to the chains. Beside him, Adam saw the same torture happening to Watch and Sally. Each had a demon on them, leering in their face. Adam's demon giggled, 'You're never going to escape!'

Adam fought to remain calm. 'Who are you? What is this place?' The town continued to change into a nightmare realm of ruined buildings and howling creatures. Up and down the street Adam could see there were many poles where poor people had been chained. Most hung lifeless, little more than skeletons, but a few still struggled to break free. The demon tugged at Adam's hair and slobbered on his shirt.

'Who am I?' the demon asked. 'I am you. I am your dark half. And this place is the Dark Corner. Those who come here from your world never return.'

'But everything looked so nice at first,' Adam said.

The demon howled. 'We always put on a show for newcomers! You humans are so stupid!'

Adam tried to sound brave, although he was in reality terrified. Most of the other prisoners he could see looked as if they had been here for ages.

'What are you going to do with us?' he demanded.

'Let you rot here until the Gatekeepers come to judge you,' the demon said. He yanked hard on Adam's head, pulling out a clump of hair. He held it up for Adam and the others to see. 'With this I can enter your world, and be you! My partners and I will pass through the Secret Path and ruin everything that is yours!'

'No!' Adam pleaded. 'Wait! We can talk about this!'

But the demon was not listening. With his partners – who had also torn off locks of hair from Watch and Sally – he put the hair in his mouth and slowly chewed it down. Then, as if by some wicked miracle, he began to change back into the form he had when they first saw him. Now he looked like Adam, and the other two demons once again resembled Watch and Sally.

'Now we have a piece of you inside us!' Adam's demon sneered. 'We're free to go where we wish!'

'You can't go into our world!' Sally shouted at the demons. 'You'll never get away with it! Our friends will spot you immediately, and you'll be destroyed.'

Adam's demon laughed in her face. 'By the time your friends know who we are they will be here with you! Rotting in the Dark Corner!'

'But maybe we can work out a compromise,' Watch

suggested. 'I can see why you don't like living here. It's a nasty place. We have ghettos back in our world that are like this. Maybe we can help you find a better place to live, and you can let us go.'

The demons howled with delight. 'We don't want to let you go!' Adam's demon said. 'We love it when humans suffer! We live for suffering! Come, my pals, let's go and play with these fools' friends!'

Adam and the others tried to stop them, but the demons danced away, heading in the direction of the cemetery and the interdimensional portal. Adam had never felt so miserable in his whole life as he did right then. It was not as if his wrists were simply chained. They were pinned above his head, and the spikes in his cuffs were digging into his skin. Of course, Watch and Sally were in equally uncomfortable positions. All round them the air filled with fumes and ash. It was difficult to breathe. Adam coughed as his throat dried. Sally hung her head as if she was about to weep.

'I'm sorry,' she said. 'It just seemed like such a nice place.'

'The demons made it seem that way so that we would drop our guard,' Adam said grimly. 'But don't blame yourself. We were fooled as well.'

'But we probably wouldn't be in this situation if it wasn't for you,' Watch added.

'That is true,' Adam had to admit.

Sally moaned. 'I said I'm sorry. What else am I supposed to do?'

'If you could reach Bryce's knapsack, we might be able to use the knife to pick these locks,' Watch suggested. It was closest to Sally. 'See if you can catch the strap with your foot.'

'I'll try,' Sally said as she strained with her right foot towards the bag. Just another few centimetres and she would have been able to reach it, but even arching her back and kicking out, the tip of her shoe kept missing the straps. After a couple of minutes of struggling she gave up. She sighed. 'I can't do it. What are we going to do now?'

'Probably rot for eternity,' Watch said.

'Don't say that,' Adam said. 'We have to maintain a positive attitude.'

'I don't know if a positive attitude helps when you're in hell,' Sally mumbled.

'We're not in hell,' Adam said. 'We're in *a* hell. That's not exactly the same thing.'

Sally stared down the street at the other captured people. A few moaned in pain. A couple even had bird's nests on top of their heads. The black ravens croaked in their dry hair. Sally sighed again.

'Right now I don't think it makes much difference,' she said.

'Look,' Adam said, trying to sound upbeat. 'We've been in difficult situations before and we've always managed to find our way out. We'll do the same this time. We just have to come up with a plan of escape.'

'We're waiting,' Watch said.

'Well,' Adam said. 'First we have to break out of these chains. Let's concentrate on that.'

'I don't think the power of our concentration is going to break these chains,' Sally said.

'I can't believe you guys are ready to give up,' Adam complained.

Watch nodded down the street. 'It looks like a tall demon is coming. I hope it's not one of those Gatekeepers the others mentioned. They didn't sound all that friendly.'

Watch was right. Another monster was approaching.

Six

'I don't know if I can go out tonight,' Cindy said. 'I think my mother wants me to stay in and babysit my little brother.'

'We'll take him with us as well,' Sally said, stepping forward. 'Enough talk. We want to go to town. We have much to do.'

'OK,' Cindy said, puzzled by their rude attitude. 'We can go back to town. Where would you like to go?'

'We need food,' Watch said. 'We need meat.'

'Do you want to go to Harry's Hamburgers?' Cindy asked.

'Yeah, let's go and get Harry!' Adam squealed.

'Let's go eat Harry!' Sally yelled.

'Eat his meat!' Watch joined in.

Cindy forced a smile. 'You guys must be really hungry.'

* * *

At Harry's her friends continued their odd behaviour. They ordered two hamburgers each, nothing else, not even drinks. Then they stopped Harry before he had begun to cook the food.

'We like our meat rare,' Adam said.

'We like it raw,' Sally added, as she grabbed one of the uncooked hamburgers and stuffed it into her mouth. In four huge bites she had eaten the whole thing. Cindy stared in amazement. Sally had not even chewed the food. She was eating as if she was, why, an animal. Cindy sat down at one of the tables and shook her head.

'What happened to you guys on the other side of the Secret Path?' she asked.

They all grinned. 'We had fun,' Adam said. 'That's all. Don't you believe us?'

'No, I don't,' Cindy said. 'Something happened to you over there. Tell me what it was.'

'What if we don't want to tell you?' Sally asked in a deadly tone.

'I don't know,' Cindy said, getting nervous. 'I'll do something. I'll talk to Bum.'

Watch came and sat by Cindy's side. He put his hand on her shoulder. He spoke with a big bite of uncooked hamburger in his mouth.

'You had better not talk about us,' he said. 'We get mad when people do that. We get very mad and then we do *things*.'

Cindy stared at him, stricken. 'What do you mean? What kind of *things?*'

Watch leaned closer. 'Horrible things,' he said softly.

Cindy's mouth quivered. 'Watch,' she said, 'what's wrong with you. You never talk this way.'

'He's talking just fine,' Sally said as she came and sat on Cindy's other side. She put a hand on Cindy's bare leg and Cindy felt as if she was being touched by a lizard. Sally stared at her with strangely bloodshot eyes. Cindy wanted to look away but found she couldn't. For a moment it seemed there was only Sally's eyes, eyes that didn't really belong to a young girl at all. It seemed that the pupils of Sally's eyes were really stone windows, that opened into a place of fire and pain. They bore into Cindy's brain, and Sally leaned over and whispered in her ear. Cindy noticed then how cold her breath was, and how it stank, just faintly, of a smell Cindy could not identify.

Out of the corner of her eye Cindy saw Adam

approach Harry, who had come around the counter, curious as to what they were up to. But Harry didn't actually make it all the way around the counter. There was a swift movement and then it seemed as if Harry sat down. Or maybe it was that he fell over, Cindy could not be sure. Suddenly she was unsure of most things. Sally spoke in her brain more than in her ear.

'We are normal,' Sally whispered. 'We are the way we have always been. You are not to talk to anyone about us. If you do talk about us, you will feel pain. We will make you feel pain.'

'Yes,' Cindy whispered back, as if from far away. A portion of her knew that her friends – if they were her friends – were trying to hypnotise her. But she lacked the will to resist. She did manage to turn her head slightly, however, away from Sally. But she just ended up staring into Adam's eyes, who now stood directly in front of her. His eyes were worse than Sally's, if that was possible. They seemed to burn with hateful red flames. He leaned close as she struggled to close her own eyes.

'You have no power to resist us,' he said in a cruel voice. 'You are under our control. You will go home now and act as if nothing has happened. But later tonight we will come for you, and take you and your little brother away.' He grinned and his mouth was full of many sharp teeth. 'We will take you to the Dark Corner.'

Seven

The demon that approached Adam, Sally and Watch was taller than the others had been, and thinner. He was also dressed differently. He wore a grey cloak instead of a furry hide, and he walked more like a man than a demon. The demons had seemed to dance and jump around like hungry animals. This demon headed straight for them as if he had important business to complete. Adam had no doubt that he was one of the dreaded Gatekeepers, and that he would soon judge them and then torture them to his heart's content.

The gang looked anxiously at each other as the demon drew near.

'Maybe we can reason with him,' Sally said.

'Like we reasoned with the others?' Watch said.

'Whatever happens,' Sally said, 'I don't want to go

first. And don't tell him it was my idea we came to this horrible place.'

'Go first with what?' Adam asked.

'With whatever he's going to do to us,' Sally said.

'Don't worry,' Watch said. 'He'll probably lower us into the boiling pit together.'

'Shh,' Adam said. 'He's almost here. Don't give him any ideas.'

The demon arrived a minute later. He stood directly in front of them and studied them up and down. His face was as ugly as the other demons, with scaly skin, a wide slobbering mouth, and piercing green eyes. He scanned up and down the street, then it seemed as if he whispered to himself.

The whispers sounded vaguely human.

'What are you three doing here?' he asked, keeping his head down.

'It wasn't my idea to come,' Sally said quickly.

'We mean you no harm,' Adam said. 'We are here looking for a friend.'

'What is this friend's name?' the demon asked.

Adam squirmed against the pole that held him bound. 'His name is not important,' he said. 'At least not to you. He's our friend. We only want to find him and leave this place.'

'Your counterparts have stolen a lock of your hair?' the demon asked.

'Yes,' Watch said.

'Then it is not easy to leave here,' the demon said. 'They have probably crossed over to your world by now. You cannot return until they decide to return here.' He paused. 'Or until they are forced to return here.'

Adam wondered at all the information the demon was volunteering. 'Who are you? Are you a Gatekeeper?'

The demon spoke in a whisper. 'I am not a Gatekeeper. But one will soon come for you. You must not let him take you. If he does, you are doomed. You will never escape from here.'

'You speak like a friend,' Watch said. 'Are you here to help us?'

The demon nodded. 'I am here to help.' As he spoke he reached up and peeled back his face, and they saw that he only wore a demon's mask. In the sober red light of the hellish realm a handsome young boy with dark hair and brown eyes stared at them.

'Bryce!' Sally exclaimed. 'I knew we would find you!'

Bryce put his finger to his lips and glanced once more up and down the street. 'Shh! Don't say my name so loudly. I am a hunted man.'

'But you're only a kid like us,' Watch said.

'Here I am a great danger to the Gatekeepers' power,' Bryce said firmly. 'I have been here almost a year, fighting their powers of darkness.'

'But I saw you last week,' Sally said.

'Time moves differently in the Dark Corner,' Bryce said. 'This is a place of pain. There is so much suffering – time passes at a crawl.'

'It's moving pretty slowly for us right now, chained here,' Watch said, trying to stretch his arms. 'Can you loosen these cuffs?'

Bryce nodded and picked up his knapsack. 'It is lucky you brought my knife and other supplies. I will be able to pick your locks.'

'Why did you leave your knapsack on the other side of the Secret Path?' Adam asked.

'I have left supplies at a dozen different portals along the Secret Path,' Bryce said, taking the knife and working on Sally's cuffs. 'I came here with another knapsack, but have since had to trade my supplies to get this disguise.'

'Who traded with you?' Adam asked.

Bryce spoke in a hushed tone. 'There are many creatures in the Dark Corner who hate the Gatekeepers. They are willing to help you, a little, if you give them something in return. But they're all scared, even the best of them. They will not risk their lives to help me escape from here.' Sally's cuffs popped open. 'That's why I need your help.'

'Was it true what you said?' Adam asked. 'That we cannot return to our world until the other demons return here?'

Bryce was grim. 'That is the rule. And none of your demons will willingly return here. They will stay in the real Spooksville as long as they can.'

'But then we're trapped here forever,' Sally moaned.

'No,' Bryce said. 'I was not tricked like you were when I first arrived here. Everyone told me to go and see my counterpart, but that just made me suspicious. I hid and tried to learn how things work here. Then I finally saw someone meet their counterpart, and I saw how the world changed after the illusion had served its purpose.' Bryce nodded down the street. 'That poor soul is chained over there. He has already been judged by the Gatekeepers, and condemned to an eternity of rotting on a steel pole.'

'Do the Gatekeepers ever let anyone go?' Watch asked.

'Rarely,' Bryce said. 'You have to be a saint to escape their judgment.' He finished opening Watch's cuffs and turned to Adam. 'My counterpart knows I'm here. He searches for me everywhere. But as long as I don't touch him, I'm safe.'

'But if he hasn't got you, can't you just leave here?' Adam asked.

Bryce shook his head. 'It's not that simple. I need my counterpart to open the Secret Path for me. That's the way it is in the Dark Corner. There is no easy way out. But I cannot drag my counterpart to the tomb. You saw how strong they are. He would just overpower me, and steal a lock of my hair, and escape to our world as your counterparts have done.'

'What are they doing in our world?' Adam asked, anxious to be free of the cuffs. Already his arms were aching.

Bryce looked worried. 'They cause pain wherever they go. It is their nature. Tell me, did you leave anyone guarding the other side of the tombstone?'

'Cindy Makey is waiting for us there,' Sally said. 'You know her, Bryce. She's that homely girl who moved here a few weeks ago.'

'She's actually very nice looking,' Adam said.

Bryce nodded. 'I know her. We must assume the worst, that the demons have already got to her.' He snapped Adam's cuffs free.

'Thanks,' Adam said. 'What will they do to her?'

'First they will try to control her mind,' Bryce said. 'Then they will bring her here, to be judged by the Gatekeepers. They will try to bring as many as possible here. They will force them through the Secret Path. They're demons – they don't have to hike all over our city to open it.'

'What can we do?' Sally asked.

'You must help me catch my own counterpart,' Bryce said. 'Remember, I can't touch him. You must overpower him and drag him to the tombstone. If his hand touches the stone, that will be enough to open the portal for me. Once I'm on the other side, I'll deal with your demons.'

'How do we know you won't just leave us here?' Watch asked.

'Watch!' Sally exclaimed. 'How can you ask such a thing. Bryce is a hero.' She paused and added, 'You really will come back for us, won't you, Bryce?'

'Yes. But I can't promise that I will be able to handle all of your demons. I can only do the best I can.' He glanced up at the sky. 'Come, it's getting dark. If you think this place is bad now wait until later. All the demons run wild at night, and they're starving. They love nothing more than to skin a human and eat him alive.'

'Sounds like a party,' Sally muttered sarcastically.

Cindy was lying in the grass by Madeline Templeton's tombstone when the others reappeared. Because she was resting with her eyes closed, she heard them before she saw them. She was surprised. They had only been gone a few minutes. She sat up when she heard them talking. They stood huddled together in front of the tombstone.

'You guys just left.' She was so relieved to see them again she broke into a huge grin. 'Did you find Bryce?'

They paused and stared at each other, as if surprised by her question. Then Adam said in a flat voice, 'We weren't looking for Bryce.'

Cindy got up slowly. 'But that's why you used the Secret Path. We talked about it before you left. Don't you remember, Sally?'

Sally broke into a smile at being addressed. She was looking round as if she had never seen the cemetery before. 'We didn't find him,' she said in a rather heavy voice. 'But it doesn't matter. We don't need him.'

Cindy was confused. 'But you were worried about him.'

'He's gone,' Watch said simply. 'He's not a problem. Take us to town.'

'What did you see on the other side of the tombstone?' Cindy asked. 'Anything exciting?'

For a moment their eyes seemed to brighten. Indeed, it was as if a faint red light shone in them. Cindy blinked her own eyes, thinking she must have imagined it.

'Would you like us to show you what we saw?' Sally asked.

Cindy shrugged. 'Yeah. If it's safe.'

Adam turned to Sally. 'We're not showing her anything right now. We have things to do here first. Later we will take her.'

'Where will you take me?' Cindy asked.

Adam smiled strangely. 'To a nice place. We will take you there tonight.'

Eight

Bryce knew where his own personal demon was. It seemed the monster was fond of hanging out at the beach. As they crept round the boulders of the jetty, they spotted him digging in the sand, searching for tiny crabs. When he would find one he would pop it in his mouth and swallow without chewing. He wouldn't even bother washing off the sand. He was an ugly little runt, but once again Bryce warned them all how strong he was.

'We can't take him by force,' Bryce said. 'Even the three of you could not handle him in his normal demonic state. You would end up all bitten and bleeding and he would just get away.'

'Do demons have a weak spot?' Watch asked.

'Yes,' Bryce said. 'They're sensitive to the cold. Notice how he doesn't actually let the water touch him, and this water is much warmer than the water at home. Cold slows them down. They're used to all the hellish fires here. What I'm going to do right now is fetch a glass of cold red lemonade. I know a place nearby where I can get it. Then one of you is going to walk by and offer it to him. Tell him that it's a glass of human blood. A demon can't resist blood. He'll gulp it down before he realises how cold it is. That should knock him out, or at least make him easier to handle.'

'How come you haven't tried this before?' Watch asked suspiciously.

'You know the answer to that,' Bryce said. 'I can't get near him. He'll recognise me. But he won't recognise any of you, not if you wear my mask and robe.'

'I'll give him the drink if the boys are too afraid,' Sally said. 'I trust you, Bryce. Did you know it was me who wanted to rescue you?'

'That's not what she wanted to tell the Gatekeeper,' Adam muttered.

Bryce wasn't interested in their group arguments. He warned them to keep his demon in sight, and keep their heads down, then he disappeared. Watch and Adam exchanged doubtful looks.

'I don't know if I trust this guy,' Watch said.

'I know what you mean,' Adam said. 'But I don't know if we have much choice.'

'What is wrong with you?' Sally demanded. 'Bryce is the salt of the earth. He rescued us once already. You should be grateful.'

'He rescued us so that we could rescue him,' Watch said. 'Once he disappears through the Secret Path we have no guarantee he's going to come back for us.'

'He himself said he's been here a year,' Adam told Sally. 'That's a long time in this kind of place. It must have changed him somehow. He might not be the same Bryce you said goodbye to last week.'

Sally was annoyed. 'Bryce is strong, inside and out. If anyone could survive here, it's him. What are you saying anyway? That he's in league with the Gatekeepers?'

'It's a possibility,' Watch said. 'The moment he's through the portal, they might jump on us.'

'Maybe he's worked out some kind of deal with them,' Adam agreed.

'Nothing changes,' Sally growled. 'You guys are jealous of him because he's so cool and competent.'

'We'll see how competent he is if he manages to get our demons back through the portal,' Watch said.

Adam sighed. 'I hope they haven't been too rough on Cindy.'

'I think the demons will be a good influence on her,' Sally said. 'Cindy needs a few rough edges to give her more personality.'

Bryce returned ten minutes later. In his hand he had a dirty glass of ice cold red lemonade. He held it out for Sally to take but now she seemed doubtful.

'How can your demon be so stupid to think a glass of lemonade is a glass of blood?' she asked.

'Demons as a whole are pretty stupid,' Bryce said. 'That's the only reason I've been able to survive here as long as I have.'

'But what if the demon only drinks a little of the lemonade?' Adam asked. 'Just enough to make him mad? He could attack Sally and hurt her.' He paused. 'I should go in her place.'

'I don't care which one of you goes,' Bryce said. 'I just need to knock this guy out as soon as possible. Remember you've got three demons running around Spooksville right now.'

'Give me your costume,' Adam said. 'Let's get this over with.'

Adam donned Bryce's demon suit and took the glass of cold lemonade. Trying to act like a normal demon out for an evening stroll, Adam walked in the direction of Bryce's demon. The monster looked up before he was halfway to him.

'Hi,' Adam called. 'Caught any good-tasting crabs?'

The demon snorted and slowly stood. He eyed Adam suspiciously. Adam was not as big as Bryce. The disguise didn't fit quite as well as it should have.

'What do you want?' the demon demanded.

'A whole bunch of human kids came through the Secret Path today,' Adam said. 'You probably heard about them. We've been over with the Gatekeepers drinking their blood. I have a glass here if you want it. I'm stuffed – I don't think I could get another drop down.'

The demon took a step closer and stared at the glass. 'Is it fresh blood?'

'Sure. Just drained it out of the fat kid myself. Have a taste, you'll love it.'

The demon was still suspicious. 'What's your name?'

'Belfart,' Adam said, remembering the name of the goblin in the witch's castle who wanted to join the Marines. The demon snorted.

'That sounds like a goblin's name,' he said. 'Where are you from? I haven't seen you round here before.'

Adam didn't believe he could stand a lengthy questioning. He decided to act more annoyed, more like a real demon.

'Listen,' he said impatiently. 'If you don't want this blood, it's fine with me.' He raised the glass to his lips. 'I'm not that full after all. I think I'll just finish it myself. Hmm – this is going to be good. Nothing like a glass of *warm* human juice in the evening.'

The demon didn't like that. In a swift move, he grabbed the glass from Adam's hand and swallowed the drink in one gulp. Then the glass fell from the demon's hand as he stared at Adam with the most peculiar expression, even for a demon.

'That must have been a cold kid,' he mumbled.

Then the demon's eyes closed and he fainted on the sand.

'Hurry!' Adam called to the others, who watched from behind the jetty.

It was almost dark by the time they were able to drag Bryce's demon to the cemetery. The demon weighed more than they would have thought for such a small guy. Watch, Adam and Sally had to do all the work. Bryce continued to maintain it was not safe for him to touch his counterpart. He told them to lay the demon beside the tombstone, but not touching it.

'He will wake up as soon as we put his hand on the portal,' Bryce said.

'You know an awful lot about demons,' Watch remarked.

'You know how everything works here,' Adam nodded.

'That's because I've kept my eyes and ears open since I got here,' Bryce said sternly. 'If you had done the same you wouldn't be in the mess you are now. You wouldn't have rushed off to meet your counterparts.'

'They sometimes make poor decisions,' Sally said quietly.

'Night's coming,' Adam said. 'How are we supposed to survive here until you return with our demons?'

'You will just have to do the best you can,' Bryce said. 'But whatever you do, try to stay round here. I can't say exactly when I'll be shoving your demons through, but you have to be right here. Otherwise you won't get back.'

'What do we do when you shove them through?' Watch asked.

'The portal will open,' Bryce said. 'You just jump through.'

'Do you know where Cindy lives?' Adam asked.

'Yes,' Bryce said. 'I'll go straight to her house and see how she is. I promise.' He nodded to his demon slumped on the ground. 'Now press his palm against the tombstone. Like I said, it will probably wake him up. You must be prepared to fight him off.'

'How do we do that?' Sally asked, suddenly not so sure about her super-hero.

'Do the best you can. I'll return as soon as I can.' Bryce paused and glanced around. 'Place his hand on the tombstone. Do it now.'

Adam did as Bryce said. Several things happened simultaneously. The tombstone glowed with a strange white light and Bryce leapt into it and disappeared, taking his knapsack with him. Then the demon was shaking his head and opening his eyes and looking angrily around.

'Hey,' he said when he saw them. 'You're the humans I heard about. You're the ones with the warm blood. Come here, I'm thirsty.'

Nine

When the knock came on the door, Cindy almost screamed. Her mother had gone out for the evening, and her little brother had a cold and had already gone to bed early. In a sense she was all alone in the house. But even though it wasn't completely dark, she was terrified to be alone. Ever since she had said goodbye to Adam, Watch and Sally, she had been trembling. They had said that they would be coming back for her. They were her friends, but just the thought of seeing them again terrified her.

And she did not know why.

She was so confused.

Her brain felt as if it was working underwater.

The person knocked again at the front door.

Cindy felt like crying. She wanted to remain silent and hope they went away. She tried that, in fact, but whoever was at the door was persistent. The knocking continued, growing harder and harder. Clutching a folded magazine for protection, foolishly, she crept to the door.

'Who is it?' she called softly through the door.

There was a pause. 'This is Bryce Poole. Are you Cindy?'

She coughed. 'What do you want?'

'I have to talk to you. It's important. Open the door.'

'No. I don't know you. Go away. Come back tomorrow.'

'I can't. This is an emergency. Your friends are in danger.'

'My friends,' Cindy muttered, not sure how she was supposed to complete the sentence. She didn't want to talk about her friends, she didn't want to see them. Yet they had told her they were coming back for her. Why did that thought fill her with dread? She saw them practically every day.

'Open the door,' Bryce demanded.

'What do you want?' Cindy asked again. 'My friends are not here.'

Again Bryce paused. 'I know,' he said quietly, so softly she almost didn't hear him through the door. 'They're trapped on the other side of the Secret Path.'

Cindy choked. 'That's impossible. I saw them.'

'It wasn't them, Cindy. It was demons who had stolen their form. Please open the door.'

Cindy finally did as she was told. Bryce practically jumped inside, and then quickly closed the door behind him. Cindy was pleased to see he was as handsome as Sally had said. Unfortunately she was not in the mood to enjoy his company. He stared at her anxiously.

'What?' she muttered.

'Look into my eyes,' he ordered.

'Why?'

'Do it!'

Cindy stared into his eyes, and as she did so the memory of staring into other eyes, much darker eyes, came back to her. Sally, Watch, Adam – they had done something to her with their stares! Cruel red flames blazed in her head, even though she felt a terrible chill in the pit of her stomach. She turned away and buried her face in her hands, tears burning her eyes.

'What is happening to me?' she said.

Bryce put a hand on her shoulder. 'The demons used their power on you. They tried to bend your will to theirs. But it's all right now. The spell is broken.'

She looked at him. 'Who are you? How do you know about demons?'

'Sally told you about me. My name is Bryce Poole. For a long time I have been exploring the many sides of the Secret Path. There I discovered many wonderful things, and many horrible things. I have just come from the worst place of them all – the Dark Corner. Your friends are trapped there now. They cannot return to this dimension until we capture their counterpart demons and force them back through the inter-dimensional portal.'

Cindy put a hand to her head. She couldn't keep up. 'I don't understand. My friends returned through the Secret Path. I saw them. I went and ate with them.'

Bryce shook his head. 'Those were not human beings who returned. They were demons. You must have noticed how strangely they acted. Even when a demon tries to hide it, his cruelty still comes out. And I know they used their eyes on you. That's why you feel so confused. But the worst of it has passed. You're free to do what you wish. You can help me if you want, and I need your help.'

Cindy had to take a breath. 'They were acting so oddly. I do remember staring into their eyes and seeing fire. But then, everything after that is mixed-up.' She paused. 'This is like some kind of nightmare. I just want to wake up.'

Bryce was grim. 'There will be no relief until we get your friends back. Tell me, what time did the demons say they would come back for you?'

Cindy strained to remember. 'I don't know. They didn't give a time. But I got the impression it would be late at night. I know there were things they wanted to do first.'

'What kind of things?'

'I don't know! If they're demons, like you say, could they hurt other people?'

A shadow crossed Bryce's face. 'They can do much worse than hurt people. They can drag them back to the Dark Corner, to the Gatekeepers.'

'Who are they?' Cindy gasped.

Bryce shook his head. 'It's better not to talk about them, not when it's almost dark.' He stepped to the window and peered out through a crack in the drawn curtains. For the first time Cindy noticed he carried a knapsack. 'We must search for them, stop them before they capture any more people.'

'Shouldn't we get help?' Cindy asked.

'No one will help us. No one will believe us. We have to do this ourselves, and we must do it now.'

'But I can't leave. I'm watching my little brother. He's asleep upstairs.'

'It's better you do leave him here. It will be safer for him. Remember, the demons want you in particular. Your brother will keep sleeping. He won't know anything is wrong.'

'But where will we look for them? They could be anywhere.'

Bryce was thoughtful. 'Each of these demons is the counterpart of one of your friends. Even though they are completely evil, they are connected to Adam, Watch and Sally. There is a good chance that they would do what those guys would do after returning through the Secret Path.'

'You mean, go home?' Cindy asked, horrified at the thought.

Bryce nodded. 'It's possible. At least it gives us a place to try to pick up their trail. Let's hurry to Adam's house. It's closest to here and Adam is the natural leader of the group. His demon probably is as well.'

'What do we do when we catch up with them?'

Bryce allowed a faint smile. 'I have studied these monsters for a long time. Don't worry, I have a few tricks up my sleeve.'

Ten

Adam was never so doubtful of Bryce as when Bryce's demon woke up and tried to attack them. Adam felt as if Bryce had set the whole situation up. Of course Adam didn't have much of a chance to be angry at Bryce. Not with the demon climbing to his feet and demanding their blood. The demon eyed Adam up and down. Adam still had his demon costume on, except for the head, which sort of ruined the effect.

'Hey,' the demon said. 'You're the one who gave me that red coloured ice-cold lemonade. That gave me a terrible headache. You owe me. Give me your arm and open your veins.'

'You think he would at least say please after making a request like that,' Sally remarked.

'Grab some sticks!' Adam yelled, reaching for a branch himself. The trouble was, in this particular dimension, there weren't a lot of stiff branches lying about. Adam came up with a stick that probably wouldn't have frightened a goblin, never mind a demon. The others fared about as well. Yet the demon seemed dismayed at their arming themselves. He continued to rub his ugly head.

'I am not in the mood to fight,' he said. 'But if you wish to surrender, I will be happy to drink your blood and bring your cursed souls before the Gatekeepers.'

'Somehow that doesn't appeal to us,' Sally said.

The demon turned away. 'Then I'm going for my partners. They'll be more than happy to fight with you, and eat you alive. Stay here until we get back.'

Adam shook his head as the demon left. 'Bryce gave us the same instruction. And it looks like it's going to get us killed, or worse.'

'You have to quit blaming Bryce for all our problems,' Sally said.

'We could blame you,' Watch said.

Adam sighed and threw down his feeble stick. 'I don't want to blame anyone. I just want to get home. But it doesn't look like we'll be able to stay here long. But if we leave we'll miss our chance to get back through the portal.'

'That is if Bryce returns with our demons,' Watch

said. 'For all we know he could be at home already, watching TV.'

'Maybe a *Twilight Zone* rerun,' Adam agreed. 'To remember us by.'

'I have faith in Bryce,' Sally said. 'If he can't save us, at least he'll die trying.'

'That should be the least he does after leaving us here,' Watch grumbled. He checked his watches. 'They've stopped. This dimension's got heavy time distortion on top of everything else.'

'We've got to come up with a plan of action,' Adam said. 'Sorehead and his friends will be back soon.' He paused. 'The only thing I can think of is to run.'

'Can demons run fast?' Sally asked.

'We're not exactly experts on demons,' Watch said.

Sally frowned. 'You're in a bad mood.'

'It must be because I'm about to be tortured to death,' Watch said. He turned to Adam. 'Where should we run to?'

'I've been thinking about that,' Adam said. 'This place is gross and disgusting but it mirrors our Spooksville in its layout. I was thinking it probably has a chapel in the same place our town has a chapel. We might be able to hide there for a while. I imagine demons would want to stay away from there.'

'But we have to time our return to this spot to match Bryce's return with our demons,' Watch said. 'And that is next to impossible with the time differences and Sorehead and his friends chasing after us.'

'We will just have to hope for the best,' Adam said, cocking his head to the side. 'Do you guys hear that?'

Sally jumped. 'Yeah. It sounds like a bunch of screaming demons, coming this way. That Sorehead sure moves fast.'

Adam began to back up. 'We'd better do the same. Let's head out the back way, and circle round to the chapel. I just hope we can make it that far.'

'I just hope the demons don't hold parties there,' Sally muttered.

Somehow they managed to make it to the chapel, but the going was rough. It was fully night now and the dark had brought about more evil changes in the town. In many places huge fissures had opened in the ground, out of which shone steaming red light. Adam, Sally and Watch thought they heard pitiful screams from these holes as they ran by.

Yet the chapel looked much as it did in normal Spooksville, perhaps a bit the worse for neglect. The place definitely needed painting and a good cleaning, but the walls and windows were reasonably intact. In fact the chapel was one of the best-kept buildings in the entire Dark Corner, and Adam felt a measure of relief. He was sure the demons could not enter the building. Hurrying inside, he locked the door behind them and hoped they would be safe for the time being.

'Maybe we should go to church more often,' Watch said, looking round.

'It would be a safer place to hang out than the cemetery,' Sally said, plopping down in one of the pews.

'But not as exciting,' Adam said, trudging towards the altar.

'I could use a little less excitement in my life,' Watch said.

Sally was astounded. 'I cannot believe you said that. The Fearless Watch, who is always ready for the next big adventure.'

Watch removed his glasses and cleaned them on his shirt. 'I am still disgusted that we will probably be tortured and eaten before dawn.'

Adam spun round near the altar and looked back at his friends. 'I hear the mob again! They're coming this way!'

It was true. The howls were growing louder by the second.

Sally jumped up. 'We have to get out of here!'

Watch put his ear to the back door. 'No. It's too late. They're already on the same street. We'd be cut down as soon as we stepped outside. We've just got to trust that they will not enter this holy building.'

'Is any building holy in this evil dimension?' Sally asked.

The demons surrounded them a minute later. Adam and his friends could see them through the stained glass windows: dozens of them, their burning torches sending shafts of wicked light across the wooden pews. Their hideous faces glaring at them with hunger. Yet in the midst of the attack Adam smiled.

'See,' he said. 'We're safe. They're afraid to come inside.'

But a minute later the gang smelled smoke.

The demons were not afraid to set the chapel on fire.

Eleven

Cindy and Bryce caught up with the demons outside Adam's house. Apparently Adam's family was out for the evening. The front door of the house lay wide open and the stereo blared on to the front lawn. The demons danced on the grass, kicking and spitting on each other as they did so. They had the radio tuned in to a heavy metal station. Cindy peered at them from round the side of the neighbouring house.

'They look like they're having fun,' she said, having doubts about Bryce's story.

'They're just getting warmed up for a night of destruction and evil,' Bryce said.

'Is it possible you're wrong?' Cindy asked. 'Maybe they weren't changed on the other side.'

'You forget,' Bryce said. 'I was with the real Adam, Watch and Sally. These are definitely impostors.' He nodded. 'See how they spit and curse each other. Is that normal?'

'For Sally it's not completely unusual.' Cindy paused and listened as the three characters giggled together. A chill went through her body and once again she saw the cold red flames in her mind. 'Never mind,' she said quickly. 'I believe you. What do you want to do?'

'We have to grab their attention and force them to follow us.' Bryce dug in his knapsack. 'We have to lead them into a place where they're most vulnerable, but a place they'll still be drawn to enter.'

'Where's that?' Cindy asked.

Bryce pulled a couple of flares out of his bag. 'A meat locker at the grocery store. Demons are always hungry for raw meat. When they see it they lose all control. They run towards it and start eating. But if they run into a meat locker, and we're able to shut the door on them and lock them inside, they'll soon pass out. Demons can't stand the cold. In fact, they'll remain unconscious for a while. During that time we should be able to drag them up to the cemetery and open the Secret Path so that we can rescue your friends.'

Cindy thought his plan was brilliant, except for a few small details. 'How do we get them to follow us into a meat locker?'

Bryce gestured with the flares. 'If we light one of these, they'll be drawn to the burning red light. It reminds them of the Dark Corner. They hate the evil realm but it's the only place they really feel comfortable.' He stopped and glanced around. 'But demons are fast on their feet. We should have bikes to keep ahead of them.'

'Adam has a bike in his garage,' Cindy said. 'Wait! He has two of them. Adam's father has more tools than Watch has. For that reason, yesterday Watch left his bike in Adam's garage. He was going to work on it tomorrow, but it's not so broken we couldn't ride it. If we sneak round the side of Adam's house, we should be able to get both bikes. There's a side entrance into the garage.'

'Good,' Bryce said. 'Then he stopped. 'But maybe you should wait here. I can do this myself. There's no reason you should risk your life.'

Cindy smiled darkly. 'My friends are in danger. That's the best reason why I should risk my life. Plus I can probably out-pedal you. None of the others can keep up with me.' She held out her hand. 'Give me one of those flares.'

'Maybe I do need you,' Bryce admitted as he reluctantly handed over one of the flares. 'You realise to get them into the meat locker at the grocery store that one of us has to run into the locker ahead of them. Then the other one will have to close the door on the demons.'

Cindy swallowed. 'And on the person inside?'

'Yes. The demons might kill whoever's inside before the cold slows them down enough to disable them. Promise me, if I get there first, you've got to shut me inside with them. You can't hesitate.'

'Will you shut me inside with them?' Cindy asked.

Bryce spoke gravely. 'I'll have no choice. It will be the only way to stop them.'

Cindy nodded weakly. 'I understand. Let's do it now, before I have too much time to think about it and get scared.'

Sneaking around the side of Adam's house and into his garage was not difficult. With the noise of the blaring stereo, the demons couldn't have heard a battalion of Marines approaching. But now came the tricky part. Bryce insisted they ride straight out the front of the garage, with at least one of the flares burning.

'We've got to pass close by them to make sure they see the burning red colour,' he said. 'It's the only way to drive them wild, and make sure they follow us.'

'What grocery store are we heading for?' Cindy asked.

'Fred's Foods. It's open twenty-four hours a day, and the place is used to unusual visitors. The Witch shops there every Friday evening.'

'You know her? We were in her castle once.'

Bryce nodded. 'I heard about that. You were lucky to get out alive.' He glanced through the garage window at the demons. 'We'll both be lucky to survive tonight. Get on that bike and get ready. I'm going to press the garage door opener. Save your flare for now. Mine should be enough to grab their attention.'

With that Bryce struck his flare. In the dark of the closed garage, the burning colour struck a knot of fear deep into Cindy's heart. How similar the light was in colour to the light that had blazed in the three demons' eyes at Harry's Hamburgers. Briefly, Cindy prayed that Harry was all right. Vaguely she remembered Adam striking him, and the man falling to the floor. Adam must be a demon to have been able to knock out a grown man.

Bryce pushed the garage door opener button.

Cindy positioned herself on Adam's bike, ready to take off.

The garage door creaked upwards.

The demons came into view.

They had stopped their dancing.

They were staring in their direction.

'Go!' Bryce cried as he shoved forward on Watch's bike.

The demons were as quick as Bryce had predicted. Even though Bryce and Cindy were on bikes and had the whole garden between them and the demons – and supposedly the element of surprise – the demons almost grabbed them as they swept by. In fact, one of the demons – it was Sally's – reached out with long nails and managed to scratch Cindy's left arm. Cindy felt a stinging sensation and then the trickle of blood over her skin. She cried out as she pedalled into the centre of the street, pushing the bike harder than she had ever pushed anything in her life. Beside her, Bryce barely kept ahead of Adam and Watch's demons. The flare burned in Bryce's right hand and the demons howled at the sight of it.

'Head for the centre of town!' Bryce called over. 'Stay ahead of me!'

'I'm trying!' Cindy called back.

'Remember what must be done!'

'I remember.' Cindy replied, but quietly, more to herself. Straining to stay a few feet ahead of the demons, she felt more afraid than she could ever remember. And the worst part was still to come. How could she close the door on Bryce and leave him to the demons' mercy?

And what if he had to close the door on her?

Ten minutes later, that looked like it might be what happened.

For some reason, after only ten minutes, Bryce's flare began to go out. It must have been defective. Cindy knew most flares were designed to burn for at least half an hour. Of course there was no time to take the thing back to the store and complain. For all she knew, Bryce had bought it at Fred's Foods. The bottom line was that she now had to strike her own flare. As she did so, the demons immediately focused on chasing her. Fortunately, just before the grocery store there was two hundred metres of downhill, and she was able to put a small distance between her and her pursuers. Bryce called over to her. His flare was all but dead.

'Throw me a flare!' he said.

Cindy glanced over her shoulder. The demons eyes burned as they had that afternoon. She had to fight not to stare into them, to be drawn into their evil depths. Inside, she could feel them willing her to slow down. She wasn't completely free of their spell.

'No!' she called back. 'There's no way you can catch it! You'll burn your hand!'

'I don't mind a little burn! Throw me the flare!'

'No! They'll get away! I'll lead them where I have to!'

Bryce stared over at her for a moment before answering. 'You can't do that, Cindy! This is my plan!'

'I'm a part of your plan!'

'No! You'll be killed!'

Cindy drew in a deep breath and pushed the bike forward as they hit the bottom of the downhill portion of the road. She replied to Bryce but not with a shout. It may have been she was simply talking to herself.

'I won't be killed,' she said.

The wind flew in their faces. The flare blazed in her hand. The demons screeched at their backs. As she neared the grocery store Cindy decided she wouldn't brake normally. Instead she would slide the bike into the front of the door like a baseball runner sliding into home plate. The move, she hoped, would gain her a couple of seconds head start for the meat locker.

But then what?

They would just chase her inside.

Bryce would just lock her inside.

The grocery store was fifty metres away now. Twenty.

Bryce began to brake.

Cindy began to tilt the bike on its side.

Her unusual strategy worked well, at least as far as allowing her to stop on a dime. The only problem was she went down with the bike, and dropped the flare in the process. She barely had time to grab it and climb to her feet before the demons ran into the car park. Bryce was only a few metres behind her, his hand outstretched.

'Give it to me now!' he shouted.

'No way,' Cindy snapped. Turning, she dashed into the store.

It was a weekday evening. The market was relatively empty. Cindy was fortunate she had been in the place before. She knew exactly where the meat section was, and therefore where the meat locker must be located. Racing down the cereal and sugar aisle, she could hear the demons shrieking at her back. They sounded both mad and excited at the same time.

Cindy dashed into the rear of the store.

She couldn't see an assistant. The meat locker stood on her right. A steel door into a wasteland of red meat. Without looking over her shoulder, too scared about what she would find, Cindy grabbed the thick handle and pulled it down and open. Inside was as dark as a cave, as cold as a bottomless well. Holding her burning flare up, Cindy strode forward. Thick slabs of beef hung all round her, like the forgotten victims of some insane war. She hurried to the rear of the freezer, and it was only then that she dared to look behind her.

The three demons stood in the doorway of the freezer.

They grinned and stepped forward.

'Hi,' the one who resembled Adam said. 'We told you to wait at home until we came for you.'

'We told you we don't like to be disobeyed,' the Sally demon said.

'We told you how we would eat you alive,' the Watch demon said.

The three of them giggled and drew closer.

Behind them, through the open door, Cindy glimpsed Bryce. Almost she shouted to him that she had made a mistake. That she did not want to be locked inside with these monsters. Almost she cried out for mercy. But the shout died in her tight throat. Bryce stared at her with sad eyes, and then he slowly shook his head. His right hand was already on the thick metal door. It seemed he closed it slowly. But maybe it was just Cindy's imagination. When the door did finally close, and the dark settled over her heart as well as her eyes, and the demons' eyes began to glow a wicked red colour, Cindy prayed to herself that it was only her imagination. That she would wake from the nightmare soon.

But the demons just kept coming closer.

Twelve

When the inside of the church transformed into an inferno, Adam and his friends were forced to flee outside. They were all choking on the smoke. Immediately they were taken captive by the horde of demons. It was Sorehead, in fact, who supervised their capture. He seemed pleased with himself now that he had them back. They were bound at the ankles and the wrists with steel cuffs. He said they were now going to be taken before the Gatekeepers and judged. Adam thought that was better than being eaten alive but after listening to Sorehead for a few minutes he had to wonder.

'You'll be brought before a judge,' Sorehead explained as he led them through the horrible night of the Dark Corner. The surrounding demons kept trying to grab them, and Adam and the others were getting tired of fending them off. Sorehead continued. 'There will be a prosecutor and you will be defended by a lawyer. There is also a jury.'

'Which is these is a Gatekeeper?' Adam asked.

'They're all Gatekeepers,' Sorehead said. 'They just change their jobs round. It gives them a little variety. Next week your lawyer might be a judge.'

'You mean, our lawyer is a demon?' Adam asked.

'Sure,' Sorehead said.

'And the jury?' Sally asked.

'Of course, they're all demons,' Sorehead said. 'You're in the Dark Corner, after all. What do you expect?'

'But how can we be judged fairly if everyone's a demon?' Adam asked.

Sorehead chuckled. 'What is this concern about fairness? We're demons. We're not supposed to be fair.' He paused and rubbed his head. 'Whose idea was it to give me the cold red lemonade?'

'It was your counterpart in our world, Bryce Poole,' Watch said.

'Where is he now?' Sorehead demanded.

'He escaped through the portal,' Adam said. 'He used your palm to open it.'

Sorehead appeared momentarily angry, but then he

laughed. 'He escaped and left you guys behind! You got to hand it to him, he's got a lot of me in him.'

'We wouldn't disagree with that,' Watch said, throwing Sally a look. But Sally, for her part, looked too miserable to defend Bryce any further.

After a mile of walking they entered one of the huge red fissures that had appeared in the ground. Travelling through a cinder-filled cave, they eventually came to a huge underground cavern. The space was surrounded at the edge by a volcanic pool. It was the glowing lava that provided the chamber with red light, and also made it uncomfortably hot. Sweat dripped off Adam's forehead, from fear as well as from the high temperature.

In the centre of the chamber was the judge, the prosecutor and the twelve demon jury. They were all resting on seats carved of black volcanic stone. The judge's seat was the tallest of all, and the judge himself was a big fat demon, with brilliant red hair and purple eyes. He was larger than most human adults. He sneered at them as they entered and Adam received the distinct impression he wasn't on their side. Beside him on his table sat a large black book.

Nearby was a massive silver-coloured scale. It was old fashioned in style, basically two balancing metal plates. Beside the far plate stood a tall thin demon. He oversaw a huge bag of thick gold coins. Adam had no idea what the scale was for, but imagined he would find out soon. Sorehead ushered them before the judge and jury, where he smacked them each on the head.

'Bow your heads to the judge and act respectfully,' Sorehead said. 'Remember, you're in a court of law.'

Just before they did bow, they each glanced over at their lawyer. He was short and chubby, and had a big cigar hanging out of the side of his mouth. His eyes were blood red and his hair was like straw that had been dipped in crude oil. He looked like a real sleaze.

'Can't we hire our own lawyer?' Sally muttered as she lowered her head.

'You can't afford one,' Sorehead. 'You should be grateful one has been appointed for you by the court. This guy's name is Foulstew, and he's not bad.'

'We should at least be given a human lawyer,' Watch grumbled, his head also lowered.

Sorehead snorted. 'He wouldn't try too hard to defend you.'

'Why not?' Adam asked, his eyes focused on the floor in front of him.

'Because we would just eat him if he won your case,'

Sorehead explained. 'We would tell him that ahead of time.'

'Silence in my courtroom!' the judge boomed, clearing his throat. 'The prisoners may approach the bench.'

Sorehead kicked each of them and they shuffled forward. They were forced to raise their heads and looked up to see the judge reading from a large piece of burnt paper.

'This trial concerns the case of the fine demons of the Dark Corner versus the wicked and ill-mannered humans of Spooksville, namely: Adam Freeman, Sarah Wilcox and Watch.' The judged paused and raised a dirty eyebrow. 'What happened to your last name, Watch?'

Watch shrugged. 'I use it so seldom, I forgot it.'

The judge turned to the thin demon next to the scale. 'A token against the accused, Scalekeeper!' he snapped.

The Scalekeeper took a golden token out of his bag and placed it on one plate of the scale. Immediately that side sunk down. Watch spoke to Sorehead.

'What does that mean?' he asked.

Sorehead was amused. 'It means you've just thrown away a valuable point. If I were you, I would watch my mouth.'

The judge pounded a gavel, which was really a skull. 'Order in the court! The charges against the accused are as follows: being human. Eating our hot dogs without paying. Escaping from the torture poles. Tricking one of our outstanding citizens with fake blood. And burning down our chapel.' The judge set aside the paper. 'How do the accused plead?'

'We didn't burn down the chapel,' Sally said. 'You burned down the chapel.'

'But you disgusting humans forced us to burn it down,' the prosecutor said, stepping forward. He was perhaps the strangest looking demon of all. He was extremely short and compact. The top of his head was flat, in fact. It looked as if a huge weight had landed on him, and simply crunched him together. His eyes were particularly wicked – they were more like a lizard's than a cat's. Worst of all, he wore a cheap wrinkled three-piece brown suit. The prosecutor continued, 'My name if Bloodbutton and it is my job to see that you each burn for your sins.'

Their own chubby lawyer with the bad smelling cigar stepped forward. 'And my name if Foulstew and I'm here to have a good time!' He laughed. 'And maybe to get you off, if you deserve your freedom, which I doubt.'

'And I'm the judge here and all of you be quiet and

let's get this trial going,' the judge said. 'How do you three plead? Innocent or guilty?'

Adam turned to Foulstew. 'How should we plead?' he asked.

Foulstew rubbed his sleazy oiled hair and took a puff on his cigar. 'If you plead guilty, you will be taken from here immediately and tortured for the rest of your lives.'

'What if we plead innocent?' Sally asked.

'You will be easily proven guilty and tortured for the rest for your lives,' Foulstew said. 'I mean, at the very least, you're obviously human. That's a serious felony in the Dark Corner. It alone carries a penalty of forty years of having your nails slowly pulled out of your hands while your toes are being tickled.'

Adam frowned. 'Isn't there a third way for us to plead?'

'Objection!' Bloodbutton shouted. 'The defendant is trying to take unfair advantage of this court.'

The judge pounded his skull. 'Overruled! You may answer your client's question, Foulstew, but please don't tell him everything.'

Foulstew bowed in the direction of the judge, and then spoke to Adam and his friends. 'It is possible for you to enter a plea of what we call Virtues versus Vices.'

'What does that mean?' Adam asked.

Foulstew nodded to the scale. 'We seat you on one end of that scale, and if you outweigh your vices – when we have finished reviewing your life – then you get to go free. For each vice we find in you, the Scalekeeper adds one of those *heavy* gold coins on to the other side of the scale. Obviously if there are too many gold coins, you will be outweighed and you will lose.'

'But what about our virtues?' Adam asked. 'For each one of those do you take a gold coin off the other side?'

Foulstew glanced at the judge. 'I ask Your Honour's permission to respond?'

The judge frowned. 'Counsel may respond. But let this court warn counsel that the jury would like at least one of these humans for dinner tonight.'

Foulstew glanced uneasily at the jury before answering Adam's question. 'That is correct. For each virtue or noble deed you are able to demonstrate in this court, one gold coin is removed from the other side of the scale. In other words, if you are a good enough person, the charges against you will be dismissed and you will be allowed to go free.'

Adam turned to Sally and Watch. 'We have led pretty good lives, for the most part. We should be able to win this way.'

'I wouldn't be too sure of that,' Sally said.

'Remember what Bryce said. You have to be practically a saint to avoid being condemned.'

'Do we have a choice?' Watch asked. 'I say we go this way.'

'Me too,' Adam said.

Sally shrugged. 'I've been as good as you guys in my days, maybe better. I'll go for it.'

Adam turned to Foulstew. 'We want to enter a plea of Virtues versus Vices.'

Foulstew looked disappointed. 'I would advise against it.'

'Why?' Watch said. 'You just said the other ways we're sure to be found guilty and be tortured for the remainder of our lives.'

'Yes,' Foulstew said, glancing at the jury of twelve demons again. 'But you probably will be found guilty this way anyway. Only this way you might get me in trouble. You wouldn't want to do that, would you?'

'We don't care if you get in trouble or not,' Sally snapped.

'What she means is we won't say anything that implicates you in our crimes,' Adam said quickly, not wishing to lose the goodwill of their lawyer.

'What crimes are those?' Watch grumbled.

'Your first crime is that of being human!' the judge

interrupted. 'Watch! Climb on to the side of the scale closest to you and sit down without moving. And keep your mouth shut.'

Watch did as he was told. Naturally, since there was only one gold coin on the other side, the scale immediately sunk down on Watch's side. That was good. If he could stay heavier than the other side, he would go free. But then the Scalekeeper raised his bag of gold coins and poured so many on the other side that the weight tilted slightly the other way. Watch bobbed up in the air. Adam and Sally were outraged.

'You can't do that!' Adam shouted. 'You haven't proven he has any vices!'

'I just said he was human!' the judge shouted back. 'That is an immediate vice of one's weight in gold. Add to that the coin Watch received for insulting me, and you can see why the scale is already tipped against him.'

Adam turned to Foulstew. 'You didn't tell me that we would have our whole weight against us before we started.'

Foulstew spread his hands. 'You didn't ask, Adam. Honestly, I am doing my best to defend you, and I am one of the best lawyers in all of the Dark Corner.'

'How many humans have you successfully defended before?' Sally asked.

'None,' Foulstew admitted. 'But I keep getting closer with each case.'

The judge pounded his skull on his desktop. 'Order in the court! It is time to weigh Watch's virtues and vices. Bloodbutton, Foulstew – prepare to present your evidence! And may the powers of darkness guide your words!'

Sally sighed and leaned over and whispered in Adam's ear. 'We're never going to get out of here.'

Thirteen

At first, as the demons closed on her, Cindy just froze. She was terrified. She could see no way out of the situation. She was locked in a dark room with three hungry monsters. She was already dinner. They would probably eat her alive.

But then she remembered the purpose of having tricked the demons into the freezer. Bryce had said the cold would eventually knock them out. Perhaps if she could delay them for a few minutes, she might give the cold long enough to do its job. They were so intent on getting her, she realised that they had not noticed that the door had been closed behind them. Cindy thrust her burning flare out in front of her.

'Stop!' she ordered. 'Or I will burn you!'

The demons giggled. Already their faces were

changing, becoming less human. Adam's demon had sprouted horns and Watch's demon had fangs. Worst of all was Sally's demon, which had snakes writhing on top of her head instead of hair. For some reason, though, at least to Cindy, the snakes did not look totally out of place on Sally's head. It was Sally's demon that first responded to her threat.

'We don't care if you burn us,' she said. 'We're used to burning. Where we come from, we burn every night.'

'Yeah,' Watch demon said. He held out his arm, and Cindy saw that it had begun to grow scales. 'Go ahead, burn my arm. Burn me a fresh tattoo. Have it say that I love human meat.'

'Raw human meat,' Adam's demon added, as he reached out with clawed hands. 'Kicking and screaming as it goes down our throats.'

'Wait!' Cindy shouted. She gestured to the sides of hanging beef. 'What about all this hamburger here? You guys had hamburgers this afternoon. You liked those pretty well. Or why don't you have some prime rib? I'll even cut you a few slices, and maybe cook you up some potatoes and onions.'

The demons looked disgusted. 'We'll eat hamburger during the day if we must,' Sally's demon said. 'But at night we like something a little more juicy.' She came a step closer. 'Like you, for example, you little trouble-maker. I think I'll eat your eyes first, and make you watch me.'

Watch's demon scowled at Sally's demon. 'If you eat her eyes first, how can she watch? She'll be blind.'

'Then I'll eat her ears first!' Sally's demon yelled.

'I get the ears!' Adam's demon shouted. 'They're my favourite piece next to the tongue. I'll eat that first and listen to her scream!'

'If you eat her tongue,' Watch's demon pointed out, 'she won't be able to scream. She won't be able to talk at all, even to tell us how much she is suffering. We should eat her tongue last.'

'I'm going to rip out her liver!' Sally demon said. 'And chew it down with a bottle of beer.' She took another step closer. 'Give me your liver!'

'Wait!' Cindy cried. 'You can't eat my liver. It will make you sick. I had hepatitis as a little girl.'

The three demons stopped in their tracks. 'Where did you get hepatitis?' Adam's demon asked quietly.

'In Mexico,' Cindy said honestly. 'When I was five years old my father took us to Cancun on vacation. You're not supposed to drink the local water but I did anyway and I got really sick. When I returned to the

States and my mother took me to the doctor he said I had hepatitis. I was sick for several weeks, and as yellow as a banana.'

Adam's demon frowned. 'What kind of hepatitis did you catch? Was it type A? Type B? Type C?'

'I don't know,' Cindy said. 'It was one of those types.'

'What difference does it make?' Sally's demon said. 'Let's just eat the rest of her and leave her liver alone.'

'It makes a big difference,' Watch's demon said. 'If she caught types B or C she could still be a carrier of the virus. If we eat her, any part of her, we might get sick.'

Sally's demon snorted. 'That's ridiculous!'

'It also happens to be accurate,' Adam's demon said.

Cindy smiled in relief. 'Yeah, you don't want to get sick. Now that I think about it, I had type B. Yeah, I'm definitely a carrier of the virus. But that's OK. There's plenty of food here. Just have one of these slabs of beef. Really, I don't mind cooking you something to go with it. I'm a great cook. In our household my mother is always working long hours and I have to do most of the cooking. I'm flexible, too, when it comes to personal requests. Any way you want your food, that's fine with me. You can have your food spicy or bland.' She added quietly, 'Just don't eat me.'

The demons looked at each other. 'She could be lying about the hepatitis,' Sally's demon said.

'If we did a blood test we would know for sure,' Watch's demon said.

'We can't do a blood test,' Adam's demon snapped. 'We're in a freezer, not a medical laboratory. Besides we're demons. We don't know how to do blood tests.' The demon suddenly stopped and glanced over his shoulder. 'Wait a second. We *are* in a freezer.'

Watch's demon put a hand out to steady himself. 'And the door's locked. That's bad. The cold's bad.'

Sally's demon swayed and pointed a claw at Cindy. 'She tricked us in here! It's her fault! Let's kill her!'

The three demons nodded in agreement and turned on her.

'No!' Cindy cried, backing into the freezer wall. 'If you eat me you'll get sick! Remember?'

'We can kill you without eating you,' Adam's demon said, now only two metres away. Ignoring her burning flare, he reached out with his gross scaly hand and grabbed her by the hair. Yet he seemed to move in slow motion and Cindy realised the cold was finally getting to them. If she could just delay a minute more, she would probably be all right. Adam's demon added, 'Do you have any final words?'

'Yes,' Cindy said quickly, stalling for time. 'Just before you kill me I want to say that it's been a pleasure meeting demons like you three. I understand you guys come from an unpleasant place and that to judge you by my standards – when I have had every advantage in life – would be completely unfair. Really, considering where you guys started, you've come pretty far. I just wanted to congratulate you.'

Watch's demon seemed impressed, although he continued to sway as he spoke, almost as if he could no longer feel his legs. 'That is awfully gracious of you. You're one of the few humans we've met who understand how difficult it is to grow up as a demon.'

'Yes, it's a hard life,' Adam's demon said, yawning heavily. 'But we try not to complain. Our motto is: "If it hurts, it can always hurt more".'

Sally's demon staggered and bumped into a side of beef, setting the red meat swaying back and forth in the gruesome red light cast by the flare. 'Enough compliments,' she said. 'Open her throat and let her bleed to death. We have to find a way out of here.'

Adam's demon nodded and moved his claw to her

throat. He tried to grip her neck, but his fingers were having trouble working.

'I'm sorry I have to do this, but we are the bad guys,' he said. 'We're supposed to do bad things. It's our nature.'

Cindy met his gaze and suddenly she did not feel afraid, although she had begun to shiver violently from the cold. 'You can't hurt me,' she said simply.

'We're not going to hurt you,' Watch's demon said, now hanging on to the wall for support. 'We're going to kill you. There's an important difference.'

'Yeah, when you're dead, you rot,' Sally's demon gasped, staggering about.

'I'm not dying,' Cindy said. 'Not today at least.' And with that she reached up and gave Adam's demon a sharp shove, and the monster toppled backwards and fell.

And he didn't get up. He couldn't.

Watch's and Sally's demons stared in amazement.

'Hey guys,' Adam's demon called from flat on his back. 'Give me a hand. This icy floor is sticking to my head.'

'Give your own self a hand,' Watch's demon snapped as he fell to one knee. 'I'm too cold to help you.'

'We have to get out of here,' Sally's demon moaned. But those were her last words because right then she collapsed where she stood, and lay unconscious. Cindy could see the others were slipping quickly under the spell of the cold. Taking a large step over Adam's demon – who didn't even try to grab her – she stepped to the freezer door and pounded on it.

'Bryce!' she shouted. 'You can open the door now!'

A few seconds later Bryce cracked the door a couple of inches and peered inside. Seeing her alive and well, he broke into a wide grin.

'Are they down?' he asked.

She glanced over her shoulder. Watch was now lying face down, and the three of them had stopped moving completely. 'Yeah,' she said. 'They're out for the count.'

Bryce opened the door all the way. 'How did you stop them from eating you?'

'I have a bad liver.'

'What?'

Cindy smiled and patted him on the back. 'It's a long story. Come, we better get these monsters up to the cemetery and get that portal open for our friends.' She paused. 'And they are *your* friends too. It's still your plan that's going to save them.'

Bryce shook his head as he stared at the frozen

demons. 'You get all the credit, Cindy. What you just did was the bravest act I ever saw in my life. I'll have to tell Sally about it.'

'She'll never believe you,' Cindy said.

Fourteen

Watch was not doing well on the scale. Incredibly, Bloodbutton seemed to have a detailed knowledge of every wrongdoing in Watch's life. Every time the demon brought one up, Watch barely bothered to defend himself. And another gold coin would be put on the other side of the scale against him.

Most of these 'sins' were small. Watch stole a cookie from the cookie jar when he was five. Watch tracked mud on the carpet when he was eight. But the way Bloodbutton related the incidents, one would have thought Watch had murdered children in their sleep.

For his part, Foulstew would prompt Watch to remember a noble deed about the time of the last related sin. However, Foulstew seemed to have no record of the good stuff Watch had done, or if he did he kept it to himself. Watch had to supply that information himself.

Finally they got up to the point where Adam had moved to Spooksville and met Watch. By then Watch was about twenty gold coins in the hole.

'Now isn't it true,' Bloodbutton said as he paced in front of Watch, 'that you talked your friend, Adam – on the very day you met him – into accompanying you on a dangerous journey on to the Secret Path?'

Watch shrugged. 'I thought he wanted to go.'

'You *thought*?' Bloodbutton snapped. 'You risked a young man's life just because you *thought* he wanted to go on such a foolish journey? Did you by chance explain to him that there was an excellent chance that he could die on this journey?'

'Bum told us all it was dangerous,' Watch said.

'Bum told him!' Bloodbutton exclaimed. 'What about you? We're talking about you here. You're the one who risked your friend's life.'

Watch shook his head. 'I don't remember.'

Bloodbutton grinned and gestured to the judge. 'Another three gold coins against the accused!'

The judge pounded with his skull. 'Scalekeeper, add three gold coins against Watch.'

Foulstew stepped forward. He glanced anxiously at

the jury and then at Watch. 'Did you do anything noble on this first journey through the Secret Path?'

Watch considered. 'I can't remember.'

'Watch,' Adam called. 'You saved my life by jumping on the back of the Black Knight in the cemetery.'

'Objection!' Bloodbutton shouted. 'That noble deed must be struck from the books! The defendant did not remember it himself.'

The judge pounded his skull. 'Sustained.'

Watch frowned. 'I saved Sally's life as well by jumping on the Black Knight's back.'

'Did you risk your life to do so?' Foulstew asked.

'I guess,' Watch said. 'The Black Knight almost killed me.'

'Objection!' Bloodbutton cried. 'Same noble deed.'

Foulstew addressed the judge. 'It isn't exactly the same deed, not technically. He was saving another person. Also, he remembered by himself that he saved Sally. No one had to tell him.' He glanced at the angry jury and added quietly, 'I think he should get some credit for it.'

The judge considered. Then he picked up the nearby big black book and leafed through the pages. The judge muttered to himself as he slobbered on the pages.

'Let's see here, what is the benefit when one human risks his life to save another human? We haven't had one of these in this court in a long time. Ah, yes, here it is.' The judge's face fell. 'Oh no.'

'What is it?' Bloodbutton asked, worried.

The judge looked miserable. 'By the rules, the defendant must be granted a credit of ten gold coins for risking his life to save another human being.'

'Ten?' Bloodbutton protested. 'That's absurd. A human's life is hardly worth a single gold coin.'

The judge glared at the prosecutor. 'Are you questioning my interpretation of the law? This is what the book says.' He spoke to the Scalekeeper. 'Remove ten coins from the balance.'

Adam whispered to Foulstew, who stood nearby. 'Who wrote that book of rules?' he asked.

Foulstew shook his head. 'It sure wasn't a demon.'

'If he gets so much credit for saving a life,' Sally said to Foulstew, 'tell him to list all the times he saved our lives.'

'I don't want to do that,' Foulstew said.

'Is it against the rules?' Adam asked.

'No,' Foulstew said. 'I'm allowed to advise him. But if you guys all get away, the jury might eat me for dinner.'

'Come on,' Sally said. 'This is a chance to win the case of your life. Even if they eat you, you'll be remembered as the greatest demon lawyer the Dark Corner ever saw. Think about that. They'll toast your exploits with blood in every demon bar in town.'

The idea seemed to appeal to Foulstew. He stepped forward, puffed on his cigar and flicked the ash in the direction of the jury. Then he addressed Watch.

'Young man,' he said. 'Jumping on the Black Knight's back was a brave act. But have you ever performed other such brave acts?'

'You mean, have I ever saved my friends before?' Watch asked.

'Careful what you say,' the judge said to Foulstew. But Foulstew seemed not to hear him.

'Exactly,' Foulstew said, glancing at Bloodbutton and smiling. 'Tell us every time you risked your life for your friends.'

'Objection!' Bloodbutton shouted.

'Shut up!' the judge shouted, leaning his bulk forward as if to hear better. 'It's too late for that. The defendant may speak.'

That was the end of that. Watch was able to list not less than a dozen times he saved his friends: with the aliens, the Cold People, the witch, the Howling Ghost, in the Haunted Cave. The list went on and on. The Scalekeeper was forced to keep removing the gold coins, and no matter how quickly Bloodbutton tried to add a few small misdeeds, the scale kept tilting Watch's way. Soon he was sitting all the way down on his side and Bloodbutton had thrown up his arms in despair.

'Bring up the next defendant!' Bloodbutton said.

The judge simmered, mainly in Foulstew's direction. 'You are free to go, Watch. But please remain in the court until your friends have been judged.'

'Thank you, Your Honour,' Watch said, climbing off the scale and flashing a rare smile.

'Adam Freeman will now step on to the scale!' the judge shouted, pounding his desk with his skull.

Adam followed a similar strategy, as did Bloodbutton at first. Going through Adam's life while Adam still live in Kansas City, Bloodbutton was able to make a significant case against Adam. Of course Adam had never saved anyone's life in his old home town for the simple reason that none of his friends had done such outrageous things that they needed to be saved. But once they got up to Adam's moving to Spooksville, Adam was able to list ten times that he saved his pals from death and at the risk of his own life. Once again he got so much credit so quickly the judge was forced to let him go. Smiling, Adam returned to where his two friends waited. He spoke to Sally.

'Just mention all the times you rescued us,' Adam said. 'We'll be out of here in no time.'

But Sally was nervous. 'But I wasn't the hero as many times as you guys.'

'Now she tells us,' Watch said.

'Sarah Wilcox to the scale!' the judge ordered.

Sally started out all right, better than the others in fact. It seemed as a small kid she had seldom misbehaved. But then when they passed her tenth birthday, Sally began to lose points dramatically. It seemed bad-mouthing another person counted for one gold coin each, and Sally had done little else for the last two years.

'Isn't it true you insulted Cindy the day you met her?' Bloodbutton demanded.

Sally stood uneasily. 'She deserved the insults. She was trying to hit on Adam and she had just met him.'

'Two gold tokens against the defendant!' Bloodbutton shouted to the judge. 'She not only committed the crime, she has no remorse about it!'

The judge pounded his skull. 'Make it three tokens, Scalekeeper!'

Naturally, Sally gained ground when her heroic

deeds were listed. Saving Cindy in the Haunted Cave from a goblin spear counted for a lot because Sally had almost taken the spear in the side. Yet as the trial began to wind down, Sally was still five tokens down and bobbing up towards the ceiling. Bloodbutton spoke about the incident with the Howling Ghost.

'So you stayed down below while your friends Adam and Cindy went up to fight with the Howling Ghost?' Bloodbutton asked.

'That's true,' Sally admitted. 'But when Adam was thrown through the wall and over the railing of the lighthouse, I was there to save him. In fact, I risked my own life when I reached out to grab him. I could have been pulled over the edge and killed.'

The judge nodded reluctantly to the Scalekeeper. 'Remove ten tokens from the scale.'

'Just a moment Your Honour!' Bloodbutton cried. 'We are not through with the Howling Ghost incident. Isn't it true, Sarah Wilcox, that when everything was over that night and everybody was safe, that you took credit for insights that Watch provided that helped Adam and Cindy defeat the Howling Ghost?'

'How do you know that?' Sally asked.

'It doesn't matter,' Bloodbutton said. 'Did you?'

Sally stammered. 'I don't understand the question?'

'Demon prosecutors don't repeat questions!' Bloodbutton yelled. 'Answer yes or no! Remember, you are under oath. If you lie, we will press your face into a boiling vat of lava this instant.'

Sally paused and looked over at Watch. 'Yes, I took credit for Watch's insight. He was the one who figured out the Howling Ghost was actually related to Cindy.'

The judge pounded his skull. 'Scalekeeper! Leave those ten gold tokens alone. A liar cannot be counted a hero.' He paused and surveyed the courtroom, picking at his nose in the process. 'Sarah Wilcox, we have completed your life review and you are found wanting. Have you anything else to say in your miserable defence?'

Sally looked as if she was about to cry. But suddenly her old toughness surfaced. She straightened herself and spoke to the entire assembly.

'I have been accused of bad-mouthing my friends and my foes,' she said. 'To these accusations I have no defence. So I did mouth off from time to time. So what? I'm a young girl. I have a right to complain. But I will say, just before being sentenced, that you demons are the sorriest looking bunch of monsters I have ever seen. You live in a dump and you smell like garbage.' She raised her voice. 'I take it as a compliment to be found guilty by a bunch of losers like you!'

Naturally, her remarks did not go down well. Bloodbutton howled for ten eternal lives of agony for Sarah Wilcox and the judge nodded his head vigorously. All the while the jury leaned forward, panting as if they couldn't wait to get their teeth into Sally. Watch kept shaking his head and Foulstew looked both relieved and disgusted at the same time. Altogether, the situation looked pretty hopeless. Then Adam shouted over the din.

'You cannot take our friend!' he yelled.

His words quieted the commotion, but the judge was smiling contemptuously. 'Your friend will be found guilty, Adam,' he said. 'Have no doubt about that. You may as well say your goodbyes now.'

The realisation finally hit Sally that she was doomed. 'Goodbye guys. Sorry I wasn't the super-hero that you were. I promise I won't ever criticise you again.'

'Soon you won't have a tongue to criticise anyone with,' Bloodbutton sniggered.

'Don't gloat over your victory,' Foulstew told him. 'It's disgraceful.'

'You cannot take our friend!' Adam repeated loudly. 'We won't let you!'

The judge chuckled and closed his black book. 'You

have no choice in the matter. Just be thankful you and Watch have managed to escape our judgment. You won't be so lucky next time.'

'We don't want to escape,' Adam said. 'We make you a counteroffer. If you release Sally, both of us will stay here in her place.'

Watch cleared his throat. 'Adam. Hmm, don't you want to discuss this?'

Adam ignored him. 'You will have both of us to do with what you want,' he said to judge. 'All we ask is that you return Sally to our world.'

'Adam,' Watch said.

Foulstew suddenly clapped his hands together. He went to shout out something but the judge silenced him with a sharp look. Once more the judge leaned over his wide desk and stared down at Adam and Watch.

'Do you honestly mean this offer?' he asked.

'Yes,' Adam said without hesitation. He bumped Watch and whispered under his breath. 'Say yes.'

'Well,' Watch said.

Foulstew hissed under his breath. 'Say yes!'

'Objection!' Bloodbutton shouted.

'Yes or no, Watch?' the judge asked.

Watch glanced round the courtroom, at the hungry jury, the evil prosecutor, the troubled judge. Finally his eyes came to rest on Sally. She continued to stand with her head bowed, looking more frail than either Watch or Adam had ever seen her before. Watch came to a decision.

'Yes, Your Honour,' he said. 'With my friend, Adam, I offer my life to save her.'

At that the courtroom went insane. Foulstew ran over to Watch and Adam and embraced them.

'There is a rule in our book,' he said, excitedly. 'If two or more people offer to give their life in our court to save the life of another, then all must go free. The rule has never been used before today, but neither the judge nor the jury has the power to overrule it.' Foulstew turned to the judge. 'Isn't that true?'

The judge was studying the fine print of the law in his big black book. 'That's true, I hate to say. Not only that. Those who have offered their lives to save Sarah Wilcox are also permitted to ask a favour of the court.'

'Objection!' Bloodbutton howled.

'Overruled!' the judge said.

'What kind of favour?' Adam asked.

The judge hesitated. 'A legal favour. It is up to you to choose it.'

Adam glanced at Watch and smiled. 'Are you thinking what I'm thinking?'

Watch nodded. 'I hate to leave any prisoners behind.'

Adam addressed the court. 'Our request is simple, but we want it carried out immediately. We want all the prisoners in the Dark Corner released. We want an end of all suffering in this dimension.'

Of course the request raised a stink.

But the court had no choice. Even the demon court.

They had to obey the rules in the book.

Epilogue

Foulstew escorted Adam, Sally and Watch to the interdimensional portal. As if on cue, Bryce and Cindy stuffed three frozen demons through the tombstone, opening the magic doorway so that they could get back to where they belonged. It was then and only then that Watch and Adam finally trusted Bryce. They could hear him and Cindy yelling on the other side to hurry and return. But Foulstew seemed sad to see them go. He handed Adam his business card.

'If you have any other legal problems in the future, be sure to give me a call,' he said.

'We will,' Adam promised, studying the card and then putting it in his back pocket. He was surprised to see the demon had a fax machine.

'Have you ever met your human counterpart?' Watch asked, curious.

'No, but I've heard a lot about him,' Foulstew said. 'He's supposed to have visited here several times. I heard he's mayor of your town, or at least he used to be mayor.'

Sally laughed. 'Bum! I should have known. You two have a lot in common!'

'Tell me,' Adam said to Foulstew. 'That book of rules you have – it really helped us out. Do you know who wrote it?'

But Foulstew just winked as he turned and walked away.

'You'll have to ask Bum that question. He's the only one who knows.'

'Ask that old worthless tramp?' Sally muttered as they got ready to return home. 'Why does he have so much secret knowledge?'

'Careful what you say about him,' Adam said.

Sally stopped and then burst out laughing. 'Yeah, I forgot already! Someone somewhere is keeping the score!'

If you enjoyed THE DARK CORNER *you'll love Christopher Pike's other Spooksville chillers . . .*

THE WITCH'S REVENGE

She's beautiful and charming.
She can be kind,
she can be cruel.
And she knows *everything* that goes on in Spooksville.

Is Ann Templeton a witch?

Sally's convinced she's evil,
but Adam and the others aren't convinced.

There's only one thing for it –
they'll have to explore the castle where she lives . . .

THE COLD PEOPLE

Why are there huge ice blocks in the forest near Spooksville? Adam and his friends are dying to know what's inside.

So they melt one – a big mistake.

A man steps out of the melting ice. He has cold eyes. An icy touch.

And he wants to turn all the inhabitants of Spooksville into Cold People.

Can Adam and the others stop him?

Look out for the next Spooksville story

THE LITTLE PEOPLE

Strange visitors have come to Spooksville.

At first they play harmless tricks – but soon the tricks turn cruel, and Adam, Sally, Watch and Cindy are fighting for their lives.

Who are these little creatures?
Why are they here?
And how can Adam and his friends make them go away?